The Best Thanksgiving Day

Written by Ann Braybrooks
Illustrated by Arkadia

☙ A GOLDEN BOOK • NEW YORK

Golden Books Publishing Company, Inc., New York, New York 10106

© 1998 Disney Enterprises, Inc. Based on the Pooh stories by A. A. Milne (Copyright the Pooh Properties Trust). All rights reserved. Printed in the U.S.A. No part of this book may be reproduced or copied in any form without written permission from the copyright owner. A LITTLE GOLDEN BOOK®, A GOLDEN BOOK®, G DESIGN™, and the distinctive gold spine are trademarks of Golden Books Publishing Company, Inc. Library of Congress Catalog Card Number: 97-80713 ISBN: 0-307-96009-9   A MCMXCVIII   First Edition 1998

One fall morning, Pooh and his friends were raking leaves when Christopher Robin said, "Today is Thanksgiving."

"What's Thanksgiving?" asked Pooh.

"It's a day we give thanks for all the good things we have and cook a big meal to share with friends," Christopher Robin explained.

Rabbit leaned on his rake. "I've had a great harvest this year," he said. "All my vegetables came up."

"I've found lots of honey this year," said Pooh.

"And I've found lots of haycorns," Piglet added.

"Then we should have our own Thanksgiving feast!" Owl said.

"Hoo-hoo-hooray!" cried Tigger, bouncing in the pile of leaves that everyone had just raked.

Quickly the friends came up with a plan.
They decided they would have their feast outdoors
in the Hundred-Acre Wood.

Kanga would set the table and make the centerpiece
while the others brought lots and lots of delicious food.
That afternoon they would all meet near Owl's house.

As the friends went off toward their homes, Tigger ran after Owl.

"Pooh's bringing honey," Tigger spouted. "And Rabbit's bringing veggibles and punkin pie. Eeyore's bringing thistles and Piglet's bringing haycorn pie. What should I bring?"

"Why don't you bring the turkey?" replied Owl.

Tigger bounced happily into the forest. "Hoo-hoo-hooray!"
he cried. "I get to invite the special guest!"

For a long time Tigger bounced through the forest searching for a turkey. He found sparrows and crows and a very cute family of quail, but there wasn't a turkey to be seen anywhere.

Finally, over by the Six Pine Trees, Tigger saw a large turkey pecking at seeds in the tall grass.

"Hallo!" he called. "Want to come to a Thanksgiving feast?"

The turkey looked up at Tigger, then whirled
around and ran away.

"Hey!" cried Tigger. "I was just trying to be nice!"

Tigger kept bouncing along, trying to find a friendly turkey. After a while he got tired, so he stopped and leaned against a boulder. Suddenly he heard a loud chorus of gobbles. It was a mother turkey and her babies!

"Hallo!" Tigger called once again, bouncing out from behind the boulder. "Would you all like to come to a Thanksgiving feast?"

At first the turkeys just stared at Tigger. Tigger smiled back
in a friendly way. Then, suddenly, the mother turkey kicked up
her feet and charged, with her babies close behind her.

"Whoa!" yelled Tigger, bouncing backward, away from
the turkeys. "Hey! What did I do wrong? What's the matter?
Haven't you ever heard about Thanksgiving?"

Tigger ran all the way to Kanga's house. As he stood outside, catching his breath, Tigger heard Roo talking to Kanga.

"Oh, Mama," Roo said. "I can't wait 'til our Thanksgiving celebration! We're going to have a turkey!"

Tigger frowned. How could he show up at the feast without a turkey now? Thinking hard, he quickly tiptoed away.

That afternoon, the friends gathered for their first
Thanksgiving feast. Kanga and Roo had set a lovely table.
Rabbit set out corn, green beans, and pumpkin pie.
Pooh licked a bit of honey from a honey pot, just to
make sure it was sweet enough.

Piglet sliced the haycorn pie.
Christopher Robin passed around freshly baked rolls,
while Eeyore gave everyone some tender thistles to munch.

"Where is that Tigger?" Owl asked. "He was supposed to bring the turkey!"

Roo pointed behind Piglet. "I see a turkey," he said.

Tigger waddled up to the table, dressed in a full-feathered turkey costume. "Since I couldn't find a turkey," he said, "I thought I'd be one."

"I'll say," Rabbit muttered with a frown. "Tigger, we need a real turkey!"

Just then the mother turkey and her babies waddled into the clearing and up to the table. They clustered affectionately around Tigger, clucking and chattering.

Tigger flapped his turkey arms and bobbed his turkey head. "I guess they decided to accept my invitation after all," he said happily. "Or maybe they think I'm their daddy."

Christopher Robin laughed. "We might as well invite your friends to share our feast, Tigger," he said. "But we'll need extra seats for everyone."

The feast began. Everyone ate and ate until even the last crumb had disappeared.

"This was a fine Thanksgiving," said Pooh as he patted his very full tummy.

And who do you think gobbled the most food of all? It was the turkeys, of course—including Tigger!